Mail Order Bride

A Bride for Thomas

Sun River Brides
Book 4

Karla Gracey

Dedication

I dedicate this book to my mother, as she was the one who kept urging me to write, and without her enthusiasm I would never written and published my books.

Contents

Chapter One

"You will marry who I tell you to marry girl." Catherine's Father towered over her, his face beet red, sweat beading his plump features.

"No I won't," she said fiercely. "You cannot make me marry Elphias Garner. He is three times my age and four times my size. I shan't do it."

"No daughter of mine will defy me. You shall stay in this house until you see sense!" He stormed from the room and slammed the door so hard that the frame wavered. Catherine sank down onto her bed and sighed. Papa had always been so indulgent towards her before. This mean spirited and angry man was not the one she loved, was not a man she recognized at all. She knew that something must have happened for him to be so frightened. But marrying her off to that venomous snake was not the answer.

She had to find a way to get Papa to tell her what was really going on, what hold the cunning money lender had over him. Her Father had not taken her Mama's untimely death well, and this was the first time in weeks she had seen him up in daytime hours. He had taken to drinking and gambling, and Catherine was sure that he had borrowed money all over town to try and run from his grief. But, she was not going to be bought and sold because of his weaknesses. She was grieving too, but she hadn't spent every penny of their family wealth.

She had to find out what he owed, and to whom. Maybe she could find a way to negotiate with them, to make an agreement as to how to make reparations? But, she knew that while Papa continued to drown his sorrows and play cards every night she would only find herself with more people to beg consideration from next week, the week after and the week after that. No, she needed to find a way to get him away from Boston. He needed a fresh start in a place where there were no memories of Mama, and no temptations from liquor and the casinos.

He couldn't stop her from going out. He wasn't around to even know, or care so his words meant little. But where should she start? Papa was out all night, every night. His study here at the house was locked tight. He hadn't been to work in months, as he slept all day, but his clerk, Andrews, sent missives every day which her Father addressed before he left the house for the evening, after a bottle of claret and some of his best port. So, she had the daylight hours to go to his place of business, and the night time to find her way into the study. She just hoped that she had the time she needed to solve the problem before she found herself wed to a man she despised and who would only ever make her life a misery.

She sat patiently opposite Papa at dinner, making polite chit chat as if their earlier argument had not occurred. She watched disgusted as he guzzled at the fine wine, and picked at the sumptuous supper Mrs Minton had prepared for them. She did her very best to bite her tongue when he brought up the subject of her impending nuptials, merely nodding and smiling as she delicately cut her steak and chewed each bite carefully. The meal seemed interminably long, and by the time her Papa had retired to take a glass of port and to smoke his cigar in his study she could barely contain herself. Why could he not hurry and leave the house? He would normally be gone in no time, his desire to lose himself in oblivion too strong.

Finally she heard the door of the study click shut from her spot in the drawing room, where she was perched anxiously on the edge of her chair. Every sinew in her body felt taut, like to break if she moved too swiftly. She listened as Papa took his hat and cane from Wilson, his valet, and tried to pick out what was being said. The two men both had deep voices, and it was hard to make out their words. She moved to the door, keeping out of sight, but she could discern no more. But, finally he was gone and she could try and explore, and see what she could do to get herself, and Papa, out of this mess.

She tried the door of the study, unsurprisingly it was locked. She wished that her upbringing had been a little less genteel, that she had a few useful skills like picking a lock, or wielding an axe. But sadly, Society deemed such skills unnecessary for a young woman. She could dance elegantly, paint a passable watercolour, and play the piano and sing at the same time. But, thankfully she was clever and she remembered that Papa never smoked without opening the window. Maybe he had left it unlatched so she could sneak in that way?

Quietly she tiptoed across the hallway, past the heavy front door and made her way towards the dining room. The French Doors led out onto a broad terrace, and Papa's study was the next room along. It would be easy for her to stand on the parapet wall and try the window. She crept stealthily across the terrace, glad that her dance lessons had taught her to be so light of foot. She gathered her skirts and tucked them up in a most unladylike fashion and clambered onto the limestone parapet. Carefully she inched towards the window, and reached out to see if it might move. It was stiff, but to her great relief it began to rise. She almost lost her footing and had to take a moment to regain her balance. Then, excitedly she squeezed herself through the open space.

Once inside she paused for a moment to catch her breath. She was sure that Wilson, or the housekeeper would be able to hear, she seemed to be gasping for air and her heart was beating faster than she had ever known. Composing herself as swiftly as she could, she made her way to her Papa's old oak rent table. His own father had brought the great monstrosity with him from England when they had come to make their fortunes some seventy years previously. Grandpa had done well, though it was rarely spoken of how a pauper lad could have turned his fortunes around so completely.

She began to rummage through the tiny drawers. When it had been made, it would have had a drawer for every tenant's home or business. Annual rents would have been marked as paid or in arrears every quarter day. Her grandfather however had not been some great landowner, quite the opposite in fact. He had been a poor tenant laborer turned poacher on the estate of an aristocrat who had turned an entire village off his land when he wished to extend the run of his game park. Hunting had been more important to him than the people who had served his family for generations. Grandpa had stolen the table from the hall, though no-one was sure how, as a symbol to himself that he would never owe his life or his livelihood to another soul ever again.

She made her way around the table. Many of the old initials had now worn away, but she knew the drawer that her Papa would keep anything of any importance in. The drawer that had, all those years before, held the rent records of Grandpa's family. Finding the drawer with a large P upon it, she hastily pulled it open and found a stack of pieces of paper. Every single one of them had her Papa's name upon it, a sum of money, and the initials I.O.U. The pile of his vowels added up to a sum greater than any she could even have imagined. They owed thousands of dollars, to people all over town. But then, she found a sheet of parchment that made her blood run cold. Elphias Garner had purchased every single one of her Papa's debts, and he had given him a very generous three months to find the money. If not, he would take the prize of his choosing. Though it did not say so in words, the meaning of the document and subsequent events were clear. Her Papa had unwittingly sold her to the highest bidder.

Well, she would not permit such a thing to happen. If even the thought of having to sell his own daughter had not been enough to change his ways, Catherine knew that nothing she could say or do would ever make one iota of difference. He would continue to rack up his debts, and would finally end up alone, and in the gutter. When she thought of the fact that he had sold her before he had considered selling their possessions, or even considered taking out a mortgage on their house told her that her dear Papa, the man who had loved her and cared for her was no more. The man left behind was a selfish drunk; a gambler who rather than gamble his own life away had gambled hers. Well, she would not stay here and let him do so. She would not watch as he drank himself into poverty at best - or an early grave at worst.

She clambered back through the window and raced upstairs to her room, where she began to grab at her clothes and possessions in a misty haze of tears. Stuffing them hurriedly into carpet bags she found under her bed and on top of the armoire she packed up her entire life in less than a half an hour. She was not sure what to do, or where she might go – but she knew she could not stay here and await the fate laid out for her, and so, bravely, she wiped away her tears, picked up her bags and walked regally down the grand staircase, as if she was daring anyone to stop her. As she reached the door, she turned and looked at the life-sized portrait of her Grandpa that hung above the mantle. "Are you proud of him?" she asked it. "Would you have sold your own child to save your own hide?"

Sadly, she was sure he would have done just that, and more. Grandpa had been a hard man, made bitter by his experiences as a poor boy, turned out of his home. He had always claimed he had done what he had to do to survive, but to hear Papa tell it, Grandpa had been proud of every time he had cheated, or gulled an innocent person along the way. She had believed that Papa was a better man, that he had done things right. Maybe he had. But Papa was not Papa anymore; she had to stop feeling that she was letting him down by trying to save herself.

She made her way down the street, not sure where she might go. The evening was cool, but not unpleasant. She walked slowly, trying to think, but her mind kept going off in different directions, making no sense of what was happening around her, to her. She walked, and walked and finally found herself at the entrance of Young's Hotel. She didn't have much money, but she had enough to get herself a room for a few nights while she tried to figure out what to do next and so she went inside.

The lobby was brightly lit, and people were hurrying around with bright smiles upon their faces. A kind gentleman at the desk took her details, and gave a large key to a lad hovering behind her. "Please take this young lady up to room four-one-six," he said as the boy took her bags and ushered her away. In minutes she was inside a luxurious room, with a large bed and a comfortable area in which she would be able to relax, with plush chairs and a table. Newspapers were stacked neatly in a rack, and a bureau stood open with good paper, pens and ink inside. Exhausted, she collapsed onto the elegant chaise longue, and smiled wanly as the boy put her bags down. "Would you like me to get one of the maids to help you unpack?" he asked.

"No, I think I would prefer to just sleep tonight. Maybe someone could bring me up some chocolate in the morning, and assist me then? Though I am not sure how long I shall be staying." He nodded and disappeared.

She pulled out her nightgown, and washed her face in the large ewer at the washstand. The bed was delightfully comfortable, and she sank into the pillows, praying she would wake up in the morning and find that it had all been a bad dream. But, despite her exhaustion, her mind would not stop spitting emotions and thoughts at her. She tossed and turned, fidgeting and wriggling in the hope that if she could get her body position just right then her mind would quiet itself – but it was to no avail. Reluctantly she got up and pulled on her robe. She took a newspaper from the rack and began to flick through it absent-mindedly. But, she soon stopped and stared. It was as if she was meant to be here, to find this simple paragraph, a paragraph she prayed would change her life.

A Gentleman of Montana seeks a woman with a view to matrimony. She should be polite and good, and not afraid of hard work. The subscriber owns a small business, in a small town, but both are growing and he needs a helpmeet. But he also longs for companionship, someone he can enjoy intelligent conversation with. A love of theatre and music would be most appreciated. Replies to

MAIL ORDER BRIDE: *A Bride for Thomas*

Box number 231, The Boston Globe

Chapter Two

Tom sifted through the mail for Sun River. Most of the farmers and ranchers nearby didn't come into the tiny town often and so he kept their correspondence for them until they could. There were a few letters for him, mostly bills, but there was one that had come all the way from Boston. He tucked it into his vest pocket, and prayed it was what he had hoped for all these weeks. He had placed an advertisement in the Matrimonial pages after seeing his friends do the same. All of them now seemed to be not just content with their mail order brides, but head over heels in love with them. He couldn't help but feel a little jealous.

The Whistling Rock Saloon had been the hub of the community for years, and he had been amongst the first folk to settle here. Back then it had been just a few trappers, and a couple of hardy souls determined to make the land yield. Few of those early pioneers were still here, but he was and his business was doing well. But, he knew he needed to make things different. In the past he had been surrounded by men. They hadn't wanted much more than a place to have a drink and play cards. But, many of them were marrying now, bringing wives and bringing up children. His back room had already been commandeered as a meeting place for the Women's Suffrage group, and was the town's place of worship when the Minister from Great Falls came to deliver a service. But with the new church that had just been erected, and the meeting hall planned for the spring, the Whistling Rock needed to change, to adapt to fit the new needs of the community – and he was full of ideas. He was also lonely, and he wanted to find the kind of happiness that always seemed to pass him by.

He finished sorting the rest of the mail and tucked each little pile into the cubbyholes he had built for the purpose, then began to check the bar over to make sure it was ready for the day's trading. He noticed that he was short on bourbon, and that the beer would only last another couple of days. He'd need to make the trip into Great Falls today to restock. He wondered if there would be anybody free to keep an eye on the place for him while he went. As if God was answering his prayers a loud hammering started up on the door. With a chuckle he unbolted it and found Ethan Cahill standing there.

"Well my friend, married life seems to be suiting you well," he teased. The young man had only been married a few weeks, and the couple had barely been seen by anyone since.

"It is mighty fine," Ethan admitted, pushing his Stetson back up off his forehead.

"What can I do for you that needs you to break down my door at this time of day? I never had you down as much of a drinker?"

"I'm not. But, I need to pick up a parcel in Great Falls and wondered if I could borrow your cart? Our gig is in no state to cope with the journey ever again!" They both chuckled at this. The gig was in fact still sitting in the street outside, the axle broken clean in two, its wheels akimbo.

"How big is the parcel my friend?"

"Maggie ordered some fabrics and some things for the bakery. I don't think it is too big. Why?"

"Well, I need to go to Great Falls myself to get some supplies for this place – but I don't have anyone to keep an eye on things while I do…"

"And you'll pick up Maggie's things if I do you a favor?"

"Something like that," he said with a cheeky wink.

"Sure, why not?" The two men shook hands warmly. "So, show me what's what my friend!" Ethan said happily. It wasn't long before Tom had shown him how to tap the barrels, how to move them so they didn't get damaged, and how to use the cash register.

"I'll be back before supper time. Things should be quiet most of the day, we get the odd few in at lunchtime, but most folk come in after supper."

"I'll be fine," Ethan assured him. "Get going, sooner you head out, the sooner you'll be back."

It didn't take him long to hitch up his broad-backed cart horses into the shafts, and soon the three of them were ambling along the road to Great Falls in the sunshine. He patted at his pocket, reassured that the letter was still there. Suddenly a wave of impatience overtook him, as he realized he couldn't wait a moment longer to find out who had responded to him. He whipped the letter out and ripped open the envelope. A second envelope fell out. The paper was fancy, a thick creamy paper and the script upon it was neat, but had a gentle slope and swirl to it. He took a quick look up, and clicked to the girls to bring them back on course, then opened it.

Dear Gentleman of Montana,

I cannot tell you how fortuitous it was that I saw your advertisement. It sounds like you could use some help, and my hands are unfortunately currently sat idle here in Boston. I would very much like to meet with you, as soon as possible, to see if we might suit – though I am sure you will have had many replies and I must not assume that I am the only woman to see something worth writing to.

I have been attending the theatre and the opera house since I was a girl. In fact, my Mama – before she so sadly passed away – was on the board of one of Boston's finest concert halls. I used to very much enjoy the opportunity to go backstage to meet with the cast, and to assist the crew, though my Mama would have been distraught to hear such a thing!

However, please do not think that I am some spoiled little rich girl, just out for an adventure. I find myself unexpectedly alone, and with only a small amount of money to my name. I do not seek your pity, nor do I expect you to consider me because of this alone. I say it merely because it is true, and for some reason writing things in a letter seems to make the telling of confidences so much easier.

I do not expect flowers and romance, I am no naïve girl. But I do believe that I would make you a good wife, one who will work hard and will support you, if you will do the same for me – as a husband of course! I long to find someone who will treat me as an equal, not as some trophy, or thing to be bought and sold. I believe I could be the helpmeet you desire.

Please, write to me soon, tell me I may use my last funds to come to Montana and meet with you at least.

Yours most hopefully

Catherine Parker

Tom stared at the page, until a jolt made him look up. Molly and Dolly had managed to wander off the road and into a small ditch. It wouldn't take much to coax them out, but he sighed heavily as he dismounted. He should have been paying attention, not been engrossed in Miss Catherine Parker's letter. Gently he helped the girls to back up, and got them back onto the road. "I'll pay more attention," he promised them as he scratched their soft, velvety mouths and then got back up onto the dashboard.

But, what he had read troubled him. He had expected to receive all sorts of things, but a woman who sounded desperate to leave Boston had not been one of those things. Clearly something had happened to her, and she felt she had to flee. But should he trust her that she was the innocent party? Was it his place to rescue a woman he had never met? It was clear she came from a wealthy family, would she even be able to cope with the kind of life he led here in Sun River? He had big plans to turn his humble little saloon into a theatre. He would need a woman not scared to set foot in either – though she had confided that she already had experience of doing so.

He couldn't stop thinking of her as they made their way into the town of Great Falls. It was much bigger than Sun River, had a railroad station, a number of banks, three saloons and a grand theatre that attracted travelling shows from Chicago and even as far as Boston and New York. He stopped outside it, and took note of everything he could see, from the shiny brass door handles to the rich red carpet inside and the tasteful show bills. He pulled out a small pad and pencil and scribbled down the names he saw on them, and wondered how he might get in touch with them.

His curiosity sated, he drove to the brewers yard where he loaded up with everything he needed, and then made his way to the station where the parcel that Ethan had asked him to collect was waiting. He stowed it carefully in the back and then turned to look at the locomotive sat puffing at the platform. Impulsively he suddenly rushed across the platform to the ticket office, where he purchased a one way ticket from Boston to Great Falls. He scribbled a hasty reply to Catherine's letter and handed it to the station master, asking him if he might ensure that it was included on the next mail run.

As he drove home, he couldn't explain to himself why he had done such a foolhardy thing. He was a man who thought about things forever, sometime to the point of never actually doing a thing. He made plans, and lists. He considered the good and bad consequences of every action – and yet he had now sent an invitation to a woman he knew nothing about. She could be some kind of criminal, or a confidence trickster for all he knew. But something told him that her distress was genuine, and he could not bear the thought of letting her down. She needed him, she needed to escape and so he would help her to do just that. If they did not suit once she got here, then so be it, but he would not leave her alone and so fearful for her future.

KARLA GRACEY

Chapter Three

Weeks had passed and Catherine's meager funds were rapidly dwindling to nothing. She had been forced to move from the smart Young's Hotel to a boarding house, recommended to her by one of the chamber maids. It was clean, but her room had few homely touches. "Catherine, I have tickets for the theatre this evening. Would you like to join me?" Gwen cried happily as she burst through the door.

"I cannot possibly afford to pay you back," Catherine admitted. "I should so love to see the new production though."

"You ninny," Gwen said affectionately. She had truly been sent to Catherine from heaven. From the very first she had taken her under her wing, and Catherine, usually so taciturn and closemouthed about her troubles, had found herself confiding in her from the start. "The concierge at the hotel gets us tickets; we don't pay a penny for them. It will be up in the God's, and standing – but a night out is a night out! They will go to waste if you will not come with me as all my friends are working tonight."

"Then I should be delighted to accompany you." Gwen smiled at her gently.

"It might help take your mind off your troubles for a short while at least. I could maybe ask if they need anyone to work at the hotel if things get too tight?"

"Thank you, but it would be too hard. Being a guest one week and an employee there soon after. It would not be right and besides, I would be too easy to find there. I have to get out of Boston, though if one of those gentlemen I wrote to does not respond I shall be stranded here."

" How many did you send letters to Catherine?"

"Twelve. I was careful, picked those that sounded the most intelligent, affluent and kind – though it is hard to tell from an advertisement of course. But, I so hope one of them will respond soon. I know it can take weeks for post to reach places such as Texas and Montana, but I had penciled into my calendar that I might be able to expect replies this week – yet there is nothing." Catherine could hear the fear and anxiety in her own voice.

"Maybe they needed time to sort through their responses and make a decision," Gwen said placating her. "I am sure someone will write and will be determined to have you join him post haste. Now, shall we dress up tonight, or down?" Catherine allowed her friend to coax her towards the little mirror above the chest of drawers. She unpinned her long chestnut locks and began to brush them out. "You have such lovely hair Catherine. You should wear it down over your shoulders more. If I had such hair I would show it off."

"I used to," Catherine said. "I fear someone might recognize me if I did so." Gwen nodded and then carefully pinned it back into an elegant chignon.

"Hmmmm," she said then ran into her room next door. Catherine gazed at her reflection, wondering if maybe she had sounded too desperate in her letters, that in her need she had scared every one of the men away. She so desperately wanted to get away from here, the memories and the possibility of bumping into her Papa, or worse Elphias Garner or one of his cronies. She simply could not bear the thought of being forced to wed that odious man. However her father had gotten himself involved with such an out and out crook she did not know, but it was not fair of him to expect her to rescue him.

Gwen arrived back with a very pretty hat. It was red, with a smart little net veil. She pinned it carefully in place. It set off the warm tones in her hair. "Well, don't you look lovely," Gwen said admiringly.

"This hat, it must have cost you a year's salary," Catherine exclaimed. "I could not possibly wear it." Gwen laughed.

"Before I was a chamber maid I was apprenticed to a smart milliner. She made hats for everyone, Madame Giradis, you may have heard of her."

"I have indeed, then this hat would have been closer to three years' salary! Everyone I knew longed to have her make them a hat. She had a waiting list so long you could make your payment now and not expect to receive your hat for an entire year. Why ever would you leave such a position to become a chamber maid?"

"Because she worked her apprentices to the bone, paid us next to nothing and slung anyone with a soupcon of talent out before they could become any kind of threat to her. I just make these for fun now. I find it soothing. And, working at the hotel can be wonderfully good fun. Well, that is until so many of my friends' have just up and left to find themselves husbands of course." Catherine heard the reprimand, though it was gently given. She was another friend who would leave Gwen behind as soon as she could.

"Why not come with me? Take your chance at finding a husband? Maybe the women out West long for smart hats to make them as fashionable as their Eastern counterparts?" Gwen chuckled at the thought.

"I doubt that many men, even out West, would be happy to have a working wife. No, I'm happy here for now. Maybe one day," she mused.

"Girls, your supper is on the table!" Mrs Ellington called up the stairs. "I shan't be joining you this evening as I shall be going out with Mr Graham." Catherine could hear the girlish hope in their land lady's voice. She had been walking out with Mr Graham for a number of months, but he had yet to ask for her hand. The doughty widow was beginning to believe she might have to start another courtship, but she didn't wish to.

17

"Good Luck," she and Gwen chorused. "He'll pop the question soon, we are sure of it." They giggled.

"Your post is by your plates girls. The door will be locked at eleven as usual, I expect you to be in before then."

"And we expect you to be in before then too," they said cheekily as they clattered down the stairs to kiss the older woman's plum cheeks and wish her a good evening.

They made their way to the table, finding a tureen of soup and freshly baked bread. The scent of the rich mutton broth made her mouth water, and Catherine ladled them out huge bowlfuls as swiftly as she could. She took a dainty, ladylike spoonful and laughed as she watched Gwen spoon hers in, in great gulps. "They will never be able to accuse me of being a lady," she admitted ruefully. "However can you be so patient? I am always half starved, cannot imagine taking such time over every bite."

"My Mama insisted. She always said that there were few things that could never be forgiven – and to eat in a way off-putting to others was one of them. It often made me wonder how she ever tolerated my Papa's table habits. He was a guzzler, but she never let on." Catherine felt a pang at the thought of those happy days before her Mama had died, when they had appeared to be a loving family with all opportunity and hope ahead of them.

"Your letter, who is it from?" Gwen asked eagerly. Catherine was so glad she had met the young woman, she was almost as invested in her finding a new home and a husband as she herself was and it felt good to have someone to care, to confide in. Catherine put her spoon down carefully and picked up the letter. Her fingers began to shake as she saw the return address was Sun River, Montana. The envelope had clearly gone to Young's Hotel, and they had neatly crossed out their details and put her new address upon it. No wonder it had taken so long to arrive if it had been reposted.

She could barely open the envelope as the tremors began to take over her entire body, a cloud of butterflies jostled for space inside her still empty belly. She had only responded to one man from Montana, that very first advertisement she had read – the one that had given her the idea of how to escape and the one she had most hoped and prayed would answer her. "I can't," she exclaimed, a tear falling onto her cheek. Gwen took her hand.

"Yes, you can. It is going to be fine, you'll see. Would you like me to do it?" Catherine shook her head, and continued to try and prise the envelope open. Finally, admitting defeat, she handed it to Gwen and wordlessly begged for her help. Gwen took the butter knife and raggedly sliced through the stiff paper. A single sheet of paper fluttered out, and a train ticket. Both women gasped as Catherine grabbed for the letter.

Dear Miss Parker

I hope you do not think me rude, but I had the strangest feeling that your letter was written in the kind of haste that could only mean one thing – that you need to escape your current situation as soon as possible. I do not purport to guess your reasons for this, and pray that we shall build up a suitably close relationship that you may choose to confide in me when you are ready. But, in all good conscience I could not let you founder without recourse to some kind of safety. I enclose a ticket which will bring you from Boston to Great Falls.

You do not have to use it, you can choose to spend some time getting to know one another through our correspondence if your needs are not as I suspect, or if they have changed. If you choose to come, I will not hold you to a marriage you may not wish for – but will offer you a position as housekeeper at the hotel I am intending to build, or as my theatre manager whichever would be your preference. I can arrange for you to stay in a boarding house, or with friends of mine should you wish to come. I don't want you to compromise anything, and we can keep it all proper and right.

I am the owner of a small saloon at present. I know this may not seem to be the most respectable of positions to a young woman of your breeding, but it is a simple place where the local people can meet. There are no girls, or any bad behavior. I would not countenance such things. The Minister preaches here every other Sunday in my back room, and many local groups meet here too – or at least they will until the new meeting hall is built. Sun River is growing so fast. We have just finished building a church, and we have a new bakery opening in town too. We have a General Store and a few specialist farm supplies places. But, I think as more and more of the farmers and ranchers marry we will see dress shops and all sorts opening too.

You didn't tell me much about yourself, but I look forward to learning more. I myself am quite a tall man and I have brown hair in need of a barber and long limbs. I will admit I have been called gangly on many an occasion! I don't often have much time for leisure pursuits, but when I do I love to read and visit the theatre in Great Falls. It was why I decided to open one here in Sun River. I think it would be mighty fine to have one closer to home.

The landscape around us here is breathtakingly beautiful and I am sure that there is the potential of attracting visitors here from across the country to see it. The air here is so healthy too, maybe Sun River could become one of those spa places that attract the sick to come and recuperate. As you may tell, I am full of ideas.

I hope I shall be meeting you from the train very soon – but if not, I would very much like to keep writing to you. You intrigue me Miss Parker.

Yours hopefully

Tom Shandon

Catherine passed the letter to Gwen and picked up the train ticket. She could hardly believe a stranger had been so perceptive as to read into her hurriedly scrawled words that she needed to escape. She kissed the ticket, and mentally wished the caress be sent to her kindly benefactor. She would be free. He didn't even demand that she wed him straight off the train. He had offered her a job, and a home. She would have loved him for those things alone – but his gentle manner and his excitement about his plans made him seem somehow youthful and full of hope. She needed such positivity to make her believe in the goodness of others once more. She had been burned so very badly by the one person she should have been able to trust with her life.

"He sounds sweet," Gwen said putting the letter down on the table. "You could leave tomorrow." Catherine could hear the sadness in her voice.

"Then we had better make tonight a night to remember," she said bravely. Gwen nodded and brushed a tear away from her eye.

"I shall miss you."

"We can write, and I'll find you a handsome Montana man to marry so you can come and join me," she teased.

"No you won't. I told you I'm not ready for that. But I'll let you know when I am."

Chapter Four

Tom paced up and down on the platform nervously. If she was coming she would be on the train. If she wasn't, then he had wasted a day. Catherine Parker intrigued him, and the longer he had to wait to get his answers the more she fascinated him. Ever since he had responded to her letter he had been unable to banish her completely from his thoughts. She seemed so worldly, yet so naïve; so capable yet so troubled. He longed to help her in whatever way she might let him.

A distant whistle told him the train was coming, and the cloud of smoke and steam that came with it engulfed him, making him choke. He waited for it to clear, not knowing whether he wished to see a young woman standing in front of him or not. Finally it began to dissipate, and he glanced anxiously at the passengers disembarking: an elderly couple, a group of young men, a widow with a small dog. None of them looked like the image he had in his mind of Catherine. Then he turned to see a young woman with her back to him. She was dressed smartly in the kind of outfit he hadn't seen except in the newspapers, nobody he knew could afford to have anything so fine. She was instructing one of the young porters to find her luggage. "I have four carpet bags," he overheard her say. "Not a trunk."

The boy scampered off and she turned.

His breath caught, and his heart began to beat so loudly he was sure she might hear it. She was beautiful. Her chestnut hair gleamed under her neat little hat, the tiny net veil doing nothing to hide her large brown eyes. She had small features, her nose tipped up a little at the end and her ears had tiny pearl studs in them. Though her travelling clothes were in a tasteful muted grey, the cut of the rich velvet hugged her slim figure perfectly, showing the curves to their fullest advantage. "Mr Shandon?" she enquired politely. Tom tried to speak, but his mouth was dry and he simply couldn't. He tried to clear his throat.

"Ahem. I am sorry," he finally managed. "Yes, and you must be Miss Parker?" She nodded. He watched as her eyes flicked up and down him. He was sure he saw a look of something approaching disappointment in her eyes, but she hid it quickly. She turned a smile on him so bright it could have lit up the entire town.

"I am so grateful to you Mr Shandon, I cannot tell you. Thank you, a million times thank you."

"Anyone would have done the same," he said flushing a little with embarrassment. He could feel the heat creeping up his neck and into his cheeks and prayed she wouldn't notice.

"No, they wouldn't – and didn't. Most people don't see what is right in front of them, so to find someone who saw what I hadn't written was a refreshing start to our relationship."

"You flatter me, but I simply sensed you needed a place to escape to – and there is none better than here."

"From the scenery I glanced from the windows of my carriage I would have to agree," she said with a smile.

"There is even more still to come," he told her and was glad to see her face light up at the thought of it. "But, we should get you home to Sun River. It is still quite a drive and I am sure you must be tired and hungry for some good food."

"Where shall I be staying?" she asked as they drove along the well worn road.

"I have arranged for you to stay with my friend Carlton and his wife Myra. She used to be a governess in Boston, I thought as you seemed to come from quite a genteel background that the two of you might have the most in common of any of my acquaintance. She is expecting a baby any day now, so could use a hand around the house so I hoped you might suit one another."

"That sounds wonderful. Do they live far from your saloon?"

"They have a farm in the valley; it's about an hour's ride from town. But, don't fret, if you don't ride yet we can soon teach you so you can come and go as you please."

"It was just that you said you wanted a helpmeet, and offered me a position working for you if we decided we did not suit - I thought I would be working with you?"

"You may do so if you choose – but I think you should let yourself settle in first, and let us get to know one another for a while." He looked into her eyes, worried she might not think it such a good idea, but she nodded.

"I think that is probably a very good idea, but I am so excited by your ideas. I should love to be a part of them if you will let me?"

"They may be some time in coming," he admitted. "I get ideas all the time, never do much about them. But I am going to have to. Things are changing here and the saloon must too. I don't want to find myself left behind."

"Then maybe I shall be the driving force you need to make you take action rather than simply plan," she said cautiously. "I am not much for dreaming. I like to make things happen."

"Then maybe we are a perfect match," he said unguardedly, then wished he had never said it. It was truly strange; he had never found it so easy to talk with anyone. But he knew he had to tread carefully. Just because he was enamored with her at first sight, did not mean that she would feel anything for him in return. He had to be patient, build her trust. He still did not know why she had run from Boston, and he was sure that was important.

Tom smiled as he watched Catherine's face fill with wonder as they drove through the snow-capped mountains, and along the wide road that was Sun River itself. The little town was just a handful of buildings, most of its inhabitants lived on farms in the surrounding valleys. "I know you said it was small, but... one, two, three...," she tailed off as she counted the number of buildings.

"Yup," he said with a grin. "Still manageable on hands right now. But just look at all the plots laid out! There'll be houses and shops on those in no time."

They continued on their way up a winding track out of the little town that turned a corner and then headed back downwards into the valley. A vast herd of cattle could be seen in the distance, and Tom could hear the calls of Mack and Ethan carrying on the wind as they herded them into the foothills for the rich grazing. "You'll be sure to meet them soon enough. Mack owns the ranch and is married to Annie, Ethan's sister. He just married a girl called Maggie. They are good people. You'll like them I'm sure. Maggie used to be a cook at Young's Hotel, where you were staying." Catherine went strangely quiet. "What is it?" he asked her softly.

"I had to leave the hotel. I couldn't afford more than a couple of nights there. But I was so lucky, my chambermaid, Gwen, she told me about the place where she boarded and there was a space there and so I had to move," she said shyly.

"Catherine, you do not have to explain anything to me unless you want to. I am not about to judge anyone because they can't afford to stay in some fancy hotel for weeks on end. I am a straightforward man, with simple tastes. Why, you saw the saloon as we went through. That has been my home for over ten years! It started out as just a tiny hut. I expanded as more people came, but it isn't exactly fancy!"

"But you have plans for it. You don't intend it to remain that way do you?"

"No I don't, but that is so I can keep a roof over my head and food in my belly. If I could leave it as it is, believe me I probably would."

"No, you wouldn't. I think there is an ambitious man inside of you

Mr Shandon. I think that is why you came here in the first place, and why you are still here too." Tom was flattered by her assessment of him. She was perceptive, and her soft brown eyes seemed to miss little. He would have to be careful around her, because he was already starting to fall for her. He just prayed that she would find something in him to care for too.

He stopped the horses outside a smart farmhouse. He watched as Catherine took in the tidy yard, the neat strips of vegetables and the beds full of flowers. Two rocking chairs sat on the porch. "This is lovely," she sighed. "Is this where I shall be staying?" He nodded and bounded up onto the stoop, where he knocked loudly on the door.

"Keep your hair on!" a friendly voice hollered. "Tom, you don't know your own strength and I'd like to keep my door where it belongs." Carlton Reed said as he opened the door, a huge grin on his handsome features. "This must be Miss Catherine Parker? Charmed."

"Thank you, and thank you for your hospitality. I would never have expected strangers to take me in, would have been happy to find a boarding house somewhere."

"Well, Myra would have none of it and I must admit I am not sure that Mrs Greig's would have been the right kind of place for a young lady. Full of miners and cowboys – chancers the lot of them," he winked at her and Tom felt his shoulders relax. They were getting on fine, and Catherine seemed happy.

"Welcome," Myra said, waddling out behind her husband. "You could have brought the tea tray for me," she said as she struggled to bend and put it down on a nearby table. "Catherine you are most welcome," she said as she kissed her gently on the cheek. "Please forgive Tom and Carlton, they weren't brought up in the world we were."

"You were a governess?" Catherine asked curiously.

"I was, to the children of Mr and Mrs Hepworth. My family was once quite well to do, nothing quite like the Parker's of course, but things changed."

"Things do – even in the hallowed halls of the Parker's," Catherine admitted.

"You must be exhausted after your travels, so have a cup of tea and then off to bed with you. I've made up the guest bedroom with clean sheets, I'm sure you'll be comfortable there."

"I shall make my excuses and leave you so you can rest," Tom said with a little bow. Carlton laughed, but kindly.

"Your customers will be thirsty too, eh?"

"I certainly hope so. Shall I come and visit with you tomorrow?" he asked Catherine. She nodded.

"Maybe you could teach me to ride so I can come and visit with you occasionally too?" she said with a smile that could just be construed as flirtatious. Tom's heart leapt in his chest, and he had to try ever so hard to hide his hopes.

"I can do that," he said.

Chapter Five

Myra soon had Catherine settled in to her room in the warm and cozy farmhouse. Her room was simple, with a heavy wooden bed and a large armoire. A washstand with a smart china ewer and matching jug meant she could freshen up before bed without having to leave the room again. She fussed around putting her things into the chest of drawers and then sank gladly onto the bed. She lay staring up at the whitewashed ceiling, marveling at how so much had changed in her life in such a short period of time.

Such a short time ago she had been living in her family's handsome town house, the respected daughter of Cornelius Parker. Her place in society had been assured. She moved in all the finest circles, enjoyed the luxuries others could only dream of. Yet in just a few tiny acts, her world had collapsed around her. She was now living in the home of two complete strangers, on the other side of America. It might as well be the other side of the world. Everything seemed so unfamiliar, yet strangely the same. The dusty tracks instead of real roads, the wooden buildings that sat higgledy-piggledy up against one another on the main street in Sun River, and this lovely farm house, and the majestic landscape it nestled within.

Tom's face drifted into her mind. He wasn't every girl's dream of handsome, but he had the kindest eyes she had ever seen and they were a shade of the softest, smokiest grey. He had not lied about being tall either. He towered over her, and even over Carlton who was by no means a short man. But she kind of liked the gangly nature of his limbs. He was endearing, and a little bit uncoordinated, with his big feet and huge hands. But he was astute and had a big heart, she was sure of that, and that made his physical imperfections fade into the dust. He was a good man, and she was beginning to wonder if he was the first truly good man she had ever known. Feeling safe for the first time in too long, she curled up under the covers and soon fell into a deep sleep.

She awoke to the sight of sunbeams dancing on the panes of glass in her window, and moved swiftly to pull the drapes to enjoy the vista before her. The valley looked even more beautiful to her in this early morning light. She could not wait to get outside and explore her new home. She hoped that Tom would come early so she could begin her education in how to be a Montana bride. She had the distinct feeling that her current skill set might be quite redundant.

She made her way downstairs cautiously. She could hear no sounds in the large house, but she was sure she wasn't the first person up. She knew that only city dwellers like her slept in past sun up. She was right; there was a note on the table waiting for her alongside a pitcher of creamy milk, some freshly baked bread and a side of ham. She poured herself a glass of milk, and carved a thick slice of the delicious looking ham. She rolled it up in her fingers and delighted in not having to use a plate or a knife and fork. She took hungry bites as she read the note that told her that Carlton was out in the fields and Myra could be found in the barn with the chickens.

She finished her breakfast quickly and headed outside to go and make herself useful. She found Myra busy scraping at a perch. "Good Morning," she said brightly.

"Should you be doing that?" Catherine asked, surely a pregnant woman should not be around such muck?

"If I don't nobody else will and then the hens will get sick, we'll get no eggs and then they'll die," she said matter of factly.

"You were truly a governess before you came here?" Catherine asked incredulously. "You seem as if you were born to this life."

"I shall take that as a compliment. I love being here, I love my husband and I don't miss Boston and its snooty folk one bit."

"I know just what you mean." They laughed together. "So, what do you know about Tom?"

"Ahh, a wise woman! He's a love," she said a slightly dreamy expression in her eyes. "Now, don't get me wrong, I love Carlton with all my heart. But Tom, well he always seems so young, in need of a bit of care and support. Not that he can't look after himself, he does. But, he has a real tender soul, would take in every waif and stray in the district. Not a bit of malice or vice in him."

"That is good to hear," Catherine admitted. His owning the saloon had concerned her a little; she did not want to marry a man like her Papa – or be employed by one. "Does he have family?"

"He's never mentioned any, but many of the men out here aren't the talkative type. It's a tough life, but they are good men. They just don't go round telling all and sundry their feelings. Now, we need to find you a riding habit, so that when he gets here you'll look the part and be all ready for him," she said excitedly.

When Tom knocked on the door, Catherine was wearing a smart pair of velvet culottes, in a burgundy red and a smart matching jacket with a light cotton blouse underneath. Considering Myra was a mite taller than her it fitted well, and she couldn't help admiring herself in the looking glass one more time before she ran downstairs to greet him.

He was wearing a Stetson, and a pair of Mr Levi Strauss's denim jeans. He looked every inch the cowboy. She felt her heart flutter a little as she took him in, and could barely speak when he bent down and kissed her lightly on the cheek. "You look lovely, quite the Montana lady," he said softly. She touched her hand to her cheek, still feeling the touch of his lips there.

"You look fine too," she mumbled.

"Shall we go and find you a horse?" he asked with a grin. She nodded. They walked over to the stable block, where three handsome looking mounts were happily chomping on nosebags full of oats. "Now, I think Midnight here might be a little too big for you and Marlin, though lovely and placid is about the strongest horse in these parts – she's happier pulling a plough than being ridden, so Emmy it is," he said as he moved to the stall of a sweet looking grey. "Now, you come here and meet her. She's a sweetie, and she loves a carrot or two." He pulled some from his pockets and gave them to Catherine. "Now, if you hold your hand just so," he showed her and then quickly adjusted the palm she showed him. Then he put the carrot in it, and she tentatively held it out towards the pretty pony.

Catherine gasped as her soft lips moved over her hand, but she could feel no teeth even though she could hear the pony happily crunching on its prize. She giggled. "That tickles," she said.

"It's kinda nice though," Tom said.

"Yes, can I do it again?" he nodded, a broad grin lighting up his face. She noticed he had the cutest smattering of freckles over his nose. It was yet another feature that had him look like an overgrown schoolboy. Tom gave her some carrots and then went to give some to the other horses too.

"I don't want them to feel left out," he said happily. She smiled. He truly was kind and straightforward. She liked that. She felt safe with him, as if he would never lie to her – and that meant more than she could ever say. "Now, it's time to show you how to put on her bridle and saddle." He lifted them down from the wall of the stall as if they weighed nothing at all. He went to hand them to her, and she dropped them immediately.

"However will she manage with that and me on top of her?"

"Horses are much stronger than they look. She's a tough little thing. Now, with the bridle, now come here, you take it in your hand like this." His big hand closed over hers and showed her exactly how to hold the mass of leather straps. "Now, you put the bit in her mouth, then swiftly pull it over her head, and make sure you don't catch her ears, she won't like that one bit." She could feel the muscles in his arm clenching against hers as he deftly maneuvered the bridle into place. Emmy twitched her ears a little, but didn't seem to be the slightest bit bothered. Tom patted her neck affectionately. "Good girl."

"Is every horse this easy?" Catherine asked.

"Nope, which is why we will leave Midnight right where he is. He can be a temperamental old soul when he wants. Emmy is a love, she'll let you make about any mistake in the book without getting riled."

"That is good, because I am already feeling a little overwhelmed."

"You'll be a natural. Just look at Myra, she came here like you – didn't know a single thing about life in the country, on a farm. But she's an excellent rider now, and manages this place so it runs like clockwork. Just give yourself time, and be patient."

"I've never been much good at patience I'm afraid," she admitted. "I like to be good at things straight away."

"Well, you shall have to curb that a little," he said playfully flicking his finger down her nose. It was the first outwardly flirtatious thing he had said or done, and she found herself fluttering her eyelashes at him just a little. He seemed to like her, and that was wonderful – because just his being so close that she could feel the heat from his lean body was doing all kinds of strange things to her senses.

The rest of the lesson in the stable went well, though Catherine was sure she wouldn't remember a thing Tom had said about how to strap the saddle on tightly or to adjust the stirrups. Her insides seemed to have turned to jelly, and she no longer wanted to learn to ride at all. All she wanted was for him to take her in his arms and kiss her until she forgot about everything that had brought her to Montana. But, he seemed determined to be a perfect gentleman, and so she found herself trying to think of ways to encourage him. Her upbringing simply hadn't covered such things. Young ladies weren't supposed to ever show desire, or even feel it. But she did, and she longed to find out more about the attraction that was building between them.

She got her chance though when they went outside and Tom took Emmy to the mounting block. Patiently he showed Catherine exactly what to do, taking each movement and slowing it down. It was funny watching his long limbs as they straddled the pony. He made Emmy look like a toy. She was nervous, he made it look so easy, but as she put her foot in the stirrup as he advised, she lost her balance. He was just behind her, and in a split second he had her cradled safely in his arms. "Whoah there," he said as she gazed up at him. "Take it slower."

"But I don't want to," she said wickedly as she pulled his head down to hers and kissed him full on the lips. He resisted, but only for the shortest moment. Then, his lips softened under hers, and he began to deepen the kiss, running his tongue gently across her mouth, encouraging her to open up to him. She was almost paralyzed by the sensations that rushed through her body. Every part of her seemed to be alive with electricity, tingling and sparking until she could hardly bear it. She snaked her arms around his body, feeling the interplay of the muscles in his back as he held her so tightly.

"Catherine, we shouldn't," he murmured against her neck, trailing kisses from her ear lobe to the collar of her jacket. "Especially not in broad daylight, in front of anyone who cares to look out."

"Myra is the only person here," she said dreamily. "She won't mind."

"But Carlton may, could come back at any moment. I don't think he would take kindly to my sullying a guest in his home."

"Sullying me?" she giggled. "If this is being sullied I wish I had learned about it much sooner. It's delicious."

"Yes it is, but you'll never learn to ride if we are both this easily distracted." She looked at him seriously.

"Hmm, you are right of course. Maybe I could ask Carlton to teach me? There'd be less chance of my being distracted then," she said outrageously.

"You are a minx. I should send you home on the first train out of here," Tom teased. She pulled away from him, a cold chill suddenly coming over every inch of her.

"You wouldn't?" she asked anxiously.

"No, of course I wouldn't. In fact I have every intention of doing the opposite, want you to marry me as soon as possible so that you can never do so."

Chapter Six

She stared at him as if he had said the most ridiculous thing in the world. Her face was pale, had blanched pure white when he had teased about sending her home. There truly was something terrible that had happened there and she was petrified of having to return. "Catherine, why did you want to run away to Montana," he asked before she could respond to his clumsy proposal. He didn't want it to be that way, she deserved romance and everything a girl could dream of.

"I didn't," she said, clumsily moving further away from him. "I just saw your advertisement and thought it might be an adventure."

"Don't lie to me, I think you applied to every man you could because you couldn't wait to get away. Now why?" Her eyes clouded over, their usual warm brown now looked almost flinty and hard.

"If I don't tell you will you send me back there? Will that mean you won't offer me a job? That you no longer wish to marry me?"

"No, of course not. But if you have any intentions of accepting my terribly timed proposal, then I want you to know I only ever wanted a true wife – one who would share everything with me, including her secrets."

"So will you tell me yours?" she spat angrily as if she expected him to keep his own past to himself. He wondered what kind of men she had known before, but he believed firmly that a relationship should be between equals. If she could accept his past, his mistakes then he could forgive hers.

"Yes, what do you want to know?" he said calmly. She sagged, and collapsed to the ground where she sat cross-legged like a little girl. He hunkered down beside her, and pulled her close, putting his arm around her shoulder.

"Why did you come here? Why do you run a saloon when you don't drink?" He chuckled.

"Ah, straight to the point. I came here because I was running away from the man I thought I might become. My Papa was an alcoholic and he was never faithful to my Mama. As a boy you want to impress your father, to make him proud and so I tried to be like him. He didn't approve of the fact that by my nature I was more like my sweet and gentle Mama. But I tried. The problem is, liquor is a demon, and soon it did have me under its thrall as much as it had ever had my father. I couldn't give it up. My Mama died, and I kept on drinking. My Papa was killed in an accident – he worked on the railroads. Accidents are common, especially to someone too drunk to notice an oncoming train." Catherine gasped, and put a hand out to comfort him. He pushed it down. "No, I don't deserve pity for that. It happened and there is nothing I can do about it now. My Papa was a fool – and I was one for treating him like a hero."

"I wasn't going to offer you pity. My Papa turned to alcohol after my Mama died too. I know it can be hard to lose someone you love, but it is so much harder to lose them when they are still alive. Alcohol is a cruel master." Her comment was pithy, but not hard. But he could sense that she had withdrawn from him a little. He could understand that, he had just admitted to using alcohol in the same way her father had, and it wouldn't surprise him if that scared her.

"It is indeed. My Papa's death woke me up to what might be my fate and I took the decision to change my life. I came out here to Montana. My hope was that as a trapper, in the wild, I would have no access to liquor and I was right. I was a terrible trapper, but the solitude and the privations helped me to move forward. I will never touch another drop as long as I live."

"I believe you," she said earnestly. Her eyes told him she believed him, but her pretty face was still pale though, and he wondered if honesty truly was the best policy. What if it meant he lost her? He had only just found her? But she had to know the truth, had to accept him for everything he was – not just the man he had become. It would not take much for him to slip backwards, he knew that. "So why the saloon?"

"Someone had to. There were growing numbers of men arriving. They wanted somewhere to congregate, to unwind after a hard day. As I said, I was a terrible trapper. Somewhere in my mind I think I convinced myself that it would be the ultimate test. If I could stay sober even when surrounded by my worst fear then I would be able to stay that way for a lifetime."

"It makes sense, I think." Catherine reached up and stroked his cheek. "You mustn't blame yourself. You achieved something many men can't, even when the most dreadful consequences are put in front of them if they do not."

"Your Father was tested?"

"And came up wanting," she said sadly. "He gambled too, and he had debts all over town. He signed a contract with a despicable man and still he couldn't pay. Elphias Garner made him sign a contract that said he could take the prize of his choosing if Papa did not pay in time. Then, out of the blue he started insisting that I marry Elphias. I can only assume that I was the prize and my dear, loving Papa was prepared to sell me to get rid of his debts once and for all."

Tom stayed silent, just letting her words sink in. He squeezed her in to his body even more tightly. He wanted her to know that he would not go anywhere, would always be by her side – but the anger inside him was raging that anyone could do such a heartless and cruel thing. He didn't dare speak. Did not want her to think he was angry at her. Finally he turned her head so that she faced him squarely. He looked deeply into her eyes. "Catherine, your Father has done you wrong and I long to take him to task for doing so. But I will not do anything without your permission. I have a question to ask, and I want you to think very carefully about it before you answer." She nodded, and stared back at him just as intently.

"Catherine, I know you still love your Father,"

"No, how could I after what he has done," she cried.

"Because he is your Father and wasn't always as he is now." She sank back against his body, tears flooding down her cheeks. She nodded and bit at her lip in her anguish. "If I could pay his debts, and bring him here to Montana and help him to give up drinking – if he wants to do so – would you want me to do that for him?"

"But he won't, he'll just take the money and gamble and drink that away again too."

"He won't get the money if he isn't prepared to get sober," Tom said adamantly. "But, if you want me to try and help him I will go to Boston and seek him out – even though every part of me longs to do him harm rather than give him a second chance."

"Oh Tom, heaven sent you to me, I am sure of it," she cried as she covered his face in kisses. "I want to hate him, but you are right. I cannot do it. I love him and I know he is still in there somewhere, we just have to find him again. I often felt that if I could just get him to leave Boston, where all his memories of Mama were, that he would be able to move forward in his grief and rebuild his life. But I had no power to make him do so."

"I think we should get you inside. You will need to rest. When I get back we will both need to be ready to be strong, if he chooses to come back with me. If he does not, then we shall have a wedding to plan – the first in our brand new church!"

"You still want to marry me?" she asked him, her little face looking so delightfully surprised that he longed to kiss her and take away all her fears.

"Oh my love, your Father's sins are not yours. Why would I love you less for telling me that you were strong and brave and did everything you could to survive such a difficult situation? You silly moppet. I think I loved you from your very first letter. I always did want to rescue a damsel in distress!" She smiled up at him, and laughed weakly. He kissed her on the forehead and then picked her up and took her inside the farmhouse.

When he came back down the stairs having deposited her gently onto her bed where she had almost immediately fallen into a peaceful sleep, Myra gave him a quizzical look. "Take care of her for me while I am gone?" he asked.

"Of course. How long will it be before we see you again?" she teased him.

"It may be a few weeks."

"Sorry?" Myra looked completely confused. "I am sure I saw two people kissing, rather passionately in my yard not half an hour ago, so much so that you seem to have quite worn poor Catherine out!"

"You did, and I did not. But that is not why I will be away. Maybe Catherine will tell you, it is not my place to do so. But, when I return I will make her my wife, whatever happens."

"What of the saloon?"

"It can stay closed, or if Ethan has the time he can open it up. I don't care." He knew his behavior was impulsive, and out of character. But, for once he knew that the more he thought about this, the less likely he would be to do the right thing, and to find out what had truly happened to Catherine's Papa. He knew alcohol, and its wiles – but it took a lot to make a happy man turn to it as a solace, even when bad things happened. Either there was something more to the story than Catherine knew, or he had always had a problem and just hidden it well.

Chapter Seven

Tom was itching with frustration by the time the grand locomotive pulled into the station in Boston. The journey had done nothing to calm his anger, but he had at least managed to make some plans as to how to go about his business. He made straight for the imposing town house that had once been Catherine's home and knocked loudly upon the grand front door. A wizened old man opened it cautiously. "You must be Wilson," he said. "I am a friend of Miss Catherine's." The man's thin lips parted in surprise, as he opened the door a little wider and ushered him in.

"Miss Catherine is all right?" he asked cautiously. "We have all been so worried for her."

"Miss Catherine is fine. I am here to try and help her father, if he will let me."

"Mr Parker has barely left his room since Miss Catherine left. He has been beside himself with worry." Tom snorted in derision. "No Sir, whatever you may have heard of him, he truly has been sick with worry. Has even stopped asking me to bring up his claret in recent days. Tom's ears pricked up at this tidbit of news. Had Mr Parker already begun to try and change his habits? He prayed it was so, for Catherine's sake.

"I must see him, whether you believe him fit to see visitors or not. I have a message from Catherine and she insisted I give it to nobody but him," he said slyly. The old butler was clearly too tired, and himself overwrought with concern for his erstwhile master, and his errant daughter.

"Come this way," he said as he began to climb the ornamental staircase that dominated the hallway slowly. He halted in front of a pair of gilded doors and nodded. "This is the master's suite," he said. "If you need anything, just ring the bell by the mantle."

"Thank you Wilson," Tom said and watched as the poor old man made his way back to wherever his duties needed him most. He took a deep breath, and knocked sharply on the door before turning the handle and marching right in.

"Mr Parker," he said in an authoritative voice. I am here on behalf of your daughter Catherine." There was no response from the great, canopied bed and so Tom moved in closer. He could hear the man's heavy breathing. It was ragged, and came in fits and gasps.

"Who are you," the grey looking man in the bed said as he came closer. His voice was husky, and quiet. Tom remembered having felt this way. The first few weeks without alcohol had most definitely been the hardest. It had felt as if he had the worst influenza, diphtheria and typhoid all at once – but there was no peaceful end in death.

"My name is Tom Shandon. I came to ask for your daughter's hand in marriage." Mr Parker raised an eyebrow.

"I doubt that," he said. "My daughter has been missing for months."

"Yes, she has been in hiding here in Boston, and recently joined me in Montana. I wish to marry her and would like your blessing," he repeated.

"If you have ever met her, which I doubt, then you would not be here asking my permission to marry her. You would be here wishing to kill me."

"Well I must admit, when she told me that you had as good as sold her to pay off your debts I did want to do exactly that. But for some reason she still loves you, wants to help you. And so, I am here to pay those debts, and to ask if you would agree to return to Montana with me. There are conditions to this offer. If you are to come with me, you must renounce alcohol for all time. I shall help you, as will Catherine to do so – but I must warn you I do run a saloon so temptation will be great."

"Why would you do such a thing? I do not deserve your sympathy, your charity."

"No, you do not. But I was once bound to alcohol myself. I know how tight those chains can be. I have managed to purge it from my life, and I know that if you wish to do so, you can too. The question I am asking you is this: is your daughter enough of a reason for you to do so? I know she hasn't been in the past, but is she now?"

"I have not drunk a drop in days," Mr Parker said wearily.

"I know, Wilson told me. But was that from choice?"

"Yes. I couldn't bear being without her, and I knew that the only way I could make it up to her was to be sober, to have paid my debts, to tell her my secrets."

"I guessed there may have been more to it than just the loss of your wife. What has been tormenting you Sir?"

"I loved my wife, more than any man should ever love another soul. She was so much fun, so sweet and everyone wanted her to be theirs. I was so proud when she agreed to be my wife. But, the delightful flirt I had fallen in love with turned out not to be just an act; she used it to gain herself a wealthy husband. You might say it was her vice, like alcohol and gambling became mine. But I loved her, blindly and stupidly. It was not until her death that I found out that she had been cuckolding me throughout our marriage. The rumors flew. I raged at them, swore my life on her virtue. But there was one man, Elphias Garner. He turned up at my place of business, with some very incriminating proof of my wife's infidelities. I could not bear for Catherine's memories of her Mama to be sullied. Did not want her to think less of her, and so I began to pay Garner to keep quiet."

"But he kept threatening to expose what he knew?" Mr Parker nodded. Tom did not want to feel pity for this man, but he had to admit it must have been a hard thing to cope with. He had lost the woman he adored, and then lost her again as he found out that she wasn't the woman he had believed her to be either.

"Indeed. Garner had known my wife, I don't think he ever knew her carnally, but he knew her better than I did. That hurt me, but I had to keep the truth from Catherine. But, a secret only ever festers, and it began to eat away at my soul - that I could tell nobody of my sadness, my loss made it that much harder to bear. Especially when Garner told me in a sneering voice that my wife hadn't been sure that Catherine was even my child."

"I think it is time for you to tell your daughter the truth Sir. She will not love you less because of other's sins. However, you still need to explain why you wanted her to marry such a man?"

"Garner kept pushing, and the more I broke the more he pushed. He waited until I had nowhere to turn, and then he sprang his little trap. I will not deny that I should never have agreed to such a thing. I should have found any way to expose him for the piece of detritus that he is, but I was so scared, and I had nothing left to fight him with. This house has been mortgaged to the hilt, I owed money to everyone I knew, my business was failing. The only thing I had left was Catherine, and in my weakness I was prepared to lose her completely, to have her hate me as I deserved to be hated rather than tell her the truth."

"The webs we weave," Tom sighed. "I think even I can forgive you in such circumstances, though you will have a lot of work to do to prove to me that your contrition is genuine. But, Catherine is good and kind, she will forgive you. She will understand, and I doubt if she will feel that the possibility you may not be her Father is anything to be concerned over. She strikes me as the kind of woman who can deal with that, and who will understand that the man who loved her and brought her up is her Papa and nobody else." The older man had tears pouring down his craggy cheeks as Tom spoke. "Now, do you think you can give up alcohol and learn not to keep secrets any longer?"

"I do, please, please take me to my daughter," he begged. Tom smiled at him.

"I will, but you will need to rest before we can undertake the journey, and I have some business to attend to with your Mr Garner."

Using the directions Mr Parker had given him it did not take Tom long to find his way to the dingy offices of Elphias Garner. The man was clearly a loan shark, and it made Tom wonder how a woman who had married someone such as Nathaniel Parker, had met him. There was more to this than Nathaniel knew, he was sure of it. But, as he entered the office a stench of decay hit his nostrils making him almost back straight out again. He looked up and down the street outside. Nobody was around, the tenements looked as if they could collapse at any minute. He went back inside, pinching his fingers over his nostrils.

He wandered through the maze of rooms, not sure what he was looking for but it was clear that nobody had been here in days. A large safe took up much of one of the little rooms, it lay open. Tom was surprised to see such a thing. A man such as Garner would surely keep both his secrets and his money locked up tightly. But, as he sifted through what was left inside he could see that other than any money that may have been in here little else had been taken. He found stacks of envelopes, each with a name printed neatly on the front, each stuffed with documents and even photographs. He rifled through them quickly and found the ones that related to the Parkers.

He leafed through the contents. In it was a record of the money Nathaniel owed him, and the money he had paid to keep his secrets. There were also details about his daily activities, and a large photograph of Catherine. Tom wondered how often the old lecher had taken it out to gaze at it, it was covered in sweaty fingerprints. But, the interesting information was inside the envelope with Catherine's Mama's name emblazoned over it. Snatching them all up, he rushed back to the town house, and began to prepare Nathaniel for his journey to Montana.

Who knew if Nathaniel would choose to stay out West with his daughter, or even if he would be able to make the changes he seemed to want to make. Tom wondered if either of the Parkers would ever see this house again, or if arranging its sale through the family's lawyers would be for the best so that they and their staff could make a new start. But Nathaniel and Catherine needed to choose whether to do that, it was not his place, though he would do whatever he could when the time came.

Epilogue

Catherine had kept herself busy after Tom had left. She couldn't stop herself from being anxious, both for her Papa and for the man she now knew she loved with all her heart. She had convinced Carlton to teach her to ride, and was now more than competent in the saddle and she had used her new found skill to ride into town and look around the place of work of her husband to be. She had taken one look at the rough wooden bar, and the dirty looking slatted walls and had decided that something had to be done. Sun River was now a place for families, and this place needed to adapt to fit that. She could see people choosing to dine here, and meet up for special occasions. But she didn't want to upset the men who might still be single and would still want a quiet place to enjoy a drink and a game of cards.

She had worked hard, whilst running the saloon as best she could, letting Ethan get on with his real work. But, she really needed Tom to come back before she began authorizing any actual building work, and so she was now kicking her heels praying for a swift return. She longed to be his wife, and for them to build a wonderful life here together. She looked up from where she was scrubbing the floor behind the bar when she heard the bell ring above the door. "Good golly," she heard a voice exclaim, one she had longed to hear for too long. "Catherine, are you in here?"

She stood up, and looked into Tom's sparkling grey eyes. She rushed out from behind the bar and flung herself into his arms. "Do you like it?" she asked as she kissed him all over his face.

"The bar, or the kisses?" he asked with a grin. "I have to admit, I love both!"

"I am so glad you are home. I think we should turn the meeting room into a restaurant. We could extend out back, to build the kitchens. We could be the first restaurant for miles. People could come to us for their birthdays, their anniversaries, their weddings…" she tailed off with a flutter of her long eyelashes.

"I take it you wish to have a big party for our wedding?"

"It would be wonderful publicity. We could invite everyone," she enthused.

"We could indeed. But, much as I love your excitement aren't you even curious as to what has been happening to me?"

"Well, Papa isn't with you, so rather than dwell on what can never be I thought it best to look to the future," she said bravely, but she could hear the emotion in her voice.

"Your Papa did come with me sweetheart, he's settling in up at Carlton and Myra's, though I think we will need to get you two a house of your own, Myra can only be days away and they'll need their peace then. I went there first, didn't expect to find you here running the saloon!"

"It is such fun. Everyone is so kind, and friendly. I feel I've gotten to know about the entire district now," she said with a grin. "He truly came? He wants to stop drinking?"

"He had already begun to before I even got there Catherine. He is so wracked with guilt. But, I think we should go home and talk about all that in privacy," he said softly, kissing her on her smooth forehead. She nodded.

"Marshall, will you be all right for the rest of the evening?" she called to a good looking lad who had suddenly appeared from out the back.

He nodded eagerly and picked up the scrubbing brush she had so recently set down. Tom looked at her quizzically.

"Who is Marshall?" he asked.

"He works for us. He's ever so diligent. He's old Henry's lad."

"You really have gotten to know everyone haven't you?" Old Henry never comes into town!"

"He's been coming since I did the place up, he says he likes it now it looks clean and hospitable." Tom shook his head in amazement as he looked back at the refurbished, and altogether more elegant, bar he now owned.

"It looks like my bar, but it truly isn't now is it?" he asked her. "With those whitewashed walls, pretty drapes and polished tables. But, I have to admit it my love, I like it!"

They rode home swiftly, and Catherine burst into the house and ran into the parlor where her Papa was sat quietly, wrapped up in a warm blanket. He was shivering still, though the fire was roaring. "Papa?" she said as she kissed him and held him tightly.

"Oh my darling," he wept. Myra and Carlton politely left the room, and Tom told her everything her father had told him. She held his hand throughout, and when Tom was finished she kissed him again.

"You poor silly man," she chided him gently. "You will always be my Papa, nobody else could ever take your place in my heart." He held her tightly and they both sobbed.

"There was something else I discovered. I don't know if it is going to make you happy or sad, or maybe a bit of both – but you should know," Tom said cautiously. Catherine looked at him, wondering what on earth he could have left out.

"I also found this file," he said as he handed over the file with her mother's name on it. "It seems that Mr Garner had been blackmailing your Mama since her marriage to your Papa. He knew she came from the tenements, was not the Society Miss she made herself out to be. He helped her to create the persona she portrayed so cleverly all her life. But, when she refused to pay him any more to keep her secrets, he threatened to make it known that she was cuckolding you, Sir.

"I don't understand? He was blackmailing me about something that was a fabrication?" Papa asked.

"Indeed, I have pored over these files carefully. He has no such evidence. He only ever showed you the envelope and the list of places he believed she had been conducting her affaires in didn't he?" Papa nodded. Catherine sat with open-mouthed astonishment at the lengths Tom had gone to for her, for her family. She truly had chosen a good man. She could never be angry with her Papa when his actions had led her here, to this clever and funny man who loved her enough to risk everything.

"Garner followed your Mama everywhere. He was a constant shadow and so he was easily able to compile lists of times when she was not seen with anyone. He knew that the inability to account for her whereabouts accurately at those times would be enough to drive you mad. He knew this, because the times he knew she was with you drove him crazy with jealousy, he was in love with her, and never forgave you for being the man who won her heart Nathaniel."

"So he wanted to punish me?" Tom nodded.

"That was why he wanted Catherine. I though this picture was of Catherine, but when I looked at it more closely, I could see that it had been handled too many times and was too faded to be Catherine, plus I know you do not have that tiny mole under your ear," he pointed to the mark on the page. "This is a picture of your Mama when she was your age." Nathaniel nodded.

"She was so beautiful."

"Yes she was, and it would seem that she never betrayed you after all. Which means, that unequivocally you must be my Papa," Catherine said delightedly. She kissed him, then stood and flung her arms around her husband. "Now, I believe we said something about getting married once you came home?"

"But what about the advertisement for the new restaurant?" he teased her.

"I don't think I can wait that long. The new Minister arrives in town tomorrow, shall we ask him to do it the day after?" He bent his head and kissed her deeply. She knew that was a yes.

The End

Thank you for reading and supporting my book and I hope you enjoyed it.

Please will you do me a favor and leave a review so I'll know whether you liked it or not, it would be very much appreciated, thank you.

Other books by Karla

SUN RIVER BRIDES SERIES

A bride for Carlton #1
A bride for Mackenzie #2
A bride for Ethan #3
A bride for Thomas #4
A bride for Mathew #5

About Karla Gracey

Karla Gracey was born with a very creative imagination and a love for creating stories that will inspire and warm people's hearts. She has always been attracted to historical romance including mail order bride stories with strong willed women. Her characters are easy to relate to and you feel as if you know them personally. Whether you enjoy action, adventure, romance, mystery, suspense or drama- she makes sure there is something for everyone in her historical romance stories!

CPSIA information can be obtained
at www.ICGtesting.com
Printed in the USA
LVHW092040280321
682767LV00024B/567